Bella and Nash

OUR FIRST CAMPING TRIP

Day 1

Kim Adams

Illustrations by
Gina Noel

Wildebeest Publishing Company, LLC
Syracuse, New York

Do you have a story to tell? What's your animal spirit? Share it with us. #hellobeesties

You may visit the author's website at www.bellaandnash.com

Wildebeest Publishing Company, LLC

For more information about copyrights and usage, special discounts on bulk purchases, workshops, and engagements, please contact Wildebeest Publishing Company, LLC at (315) 220-0217, info@ wildebeestpublishing.com, or online at www.wildebeestpublishing.com Wildebeest Publishing is dedicated to providing flexible remote work opportunities and has a presence in Syracuse, New York City, Tampa, and Denver.

Wildebeest Publishing Company, LLC, paperback, First Edition December 2025, United States of America

Illustrations by Gina Noel

ISBN 978-1-958233-48-1 (paperback)
ISBN 978-1-958233-49-8 (ebook)
LLCN 2025916552

For all the students I've taught throughout my career.
I learned so much from you. Thank you!
Kim

For my husband, children, and grandchildren. I love you.
Gina

Table of Contents

Chapter 1

Morning Excitement

BEEP BEEP BEEP

Normally, there are no alarms during summer vacation, but today is special. I'm taking my very first camping trip with my grandfather. Pop Pop, or Pop, I call him. Pop is my dad's father. Dad packed some clothes and camping gear for me last night, but I wonder what else I may need. Dashing between my room and the bathroom, I grab my favorite pink hoodie and my writing journal.

"Don't forget your toothbrush," Dad hollered from the bottom of the stairs.

"Okay," I replied.

After quickly brushing my teeth, I wrapped my pink toothbrush in a tissue and slipped it into my backpack. I snatched the Winnie-the-Pooh stuffed bear my mom gave me years ago. I put Pooh in my backpack, too. Pooh was her favorite stuffed animal when she was a kid. He's alright, but I only sleep with him because it reminds me of her. Vivid thoughts moisten my eyes. I see her, but not here in the house. She's on my mind. Less than a year ago, that DUMB cancer stole her from me.

"Get your sweatshirt and boots," Dad shouted up to me. "It's cold in the mountains at night!"

"Got them!" I shouted back.

Dad has to remember a lot and do everything for me that my mother used to, and he's doing pretty good, except for that one time my white T-shirt turned pink after he washed it. It was a memorable laundry day!

"Bella, it's okay," he assured me as he handed it over. Fortunately, I wasn't too mad since I *really* like pink. Actually, it's my favorite color in the whole wide world!

Bella. That's me! My name is Isabella Rose. **Everybody,** even my teachers, calls me Bella. Bella means beautiful.

I was named after my two great-grandmothers. Grandma Isabella and Nonna Rose. Nonna means grandmother in Italian. My mother's grandmother was Isabella, and my father's grandmother's name was Rose. I never met them. They are both deceased. That means dead. Like my mother.

We're Italian American, and my Nonna Elizabeth said that I should be proud of my name and heritage. The names Isabella and Elizabeth are very similar. Nonna Elizabeth can tell you the history of both if you ask her. She is my Pop's wife.

I look like my mother. My eyes are dark brown, and I have long black hair that's always pulled back in a pony-tail. Ponytail. That word makes me laugh.

Here's another fact about me: I can hold my breath underwater for a really long time, but I'm not a great swim-mer. I took lessons when I was little, but unless I can feel my feet touch the bottom of a pool, I freak out. Really freak out! Like … I hyperventilate and everything! The shallow end is *always* where I swim.

In September, I'll be in Fourth Grade. I'm nine years old, but I can't wait until I'm ten because Dad said that I can get my very own cell phone when I turn ten! I cried and begged, trying to convince him that every kid at school has them. Well, almost every kid — I lied. I told him that I **absolutely** should, too, but my crying didn't work. Dad is sticking to that (magical — he calls it) number of age ten because he said that's what he and Mom had decided years ago. He's always saying things like that.

I bounded down the stairs to the kitchen, where Dad's standing, drinking a cup of coffee. He's tall with short dark hair.

"Bella, you have to eat something before you leave," he insisted.

"I'm not hungry," I refused, pretending to be a kangaroo. Doesn't he notice that I'm too excited to eat?

"Where's Pop?" I asked, bouncing on two feet and ready with lots more questions for Dad. "He should be here by now."

"He's on his way."

"So. Where are we going camping?"

"The Adirondacks."

"Adirondacks? What's an Adirondack?"

"They're a mountain range right here in New York State. Miles and miles of land called The Adirondack Park." Dad said, walking into the family room, "It's called The Adirondacks."

He returned with some folded-up paper.

Now I'm curious. "What's that?" I asked.

"It's a New York State map," he said.

He unfolded it and opened it on the counter, and it got bigger and bigger like some sort of magic trick.

"Oh, we learned about maps in school," I said, excited.

"Yes, and this school year you're going to learn all about New York State," he said.

My mom was a teacher. She knew the topics that were covered for each grade in elementary school. She must have told him.

"Okay. This is a road map," Dad explained, "Do you see all of the red, green, yellow, and black colored lines? They are all different roads and highways. The blue color shows the lakes and rivers."

"Why don't you just use the map on your phone?" I asked.

"Because I want **you** to be able to bring this on the trip with you!" He sighed.

I'm looking, and he's reading the map to me. Reading. My mom said that's how you can learn more. Reading teaches you about anything that interests you and new vocabulary words, too. That's why I'm smart. I love to read! I'm an **excellent** student. That's what's written on my report cards. All **Es**. E stands for EXCEEDS EXPECTATIONS. I also get hundreds on my spelling, grammar, and comprehension tests. I don't really care for math. All of that showing your work, labeling, and writing out the answers is exhausting. Then I have to do it on the laptop, too!

During that COVID year, when the schools shut down, and every kid had to learn remotely, my mother taught her class from our home. She was on her computer all day, making sure her students understood what she was teaching them. She used to say that she didn't want me to fall behind, so I completed the ELA (that stands for English Language Arts — which is basically reading and writing) along with math, science, and social studies assignments.

When I didn't understand something that my teacher was teaching, Mom patiently explained it to me. If she got too busy to check on me during the day, she made me do my work after dinner at night. I didn't like it, but I guess I was lucky that my mom was a teacher.

Some of my friends were not as fortunate, and their parents had to become teachers! I **hated** remote learning. I liked being at home with my mother, but I couldn't see my friends from school. The only friend I saw was my next-door neighbor, Steffi. We had to play outside because our mothers didn't want us to catch any illness from each other. Her name is Stephanie, but her family calls her Steffi, and so do I. I've known her since we were four, when her family moved from Albany.

"All of the white is land," Dad pointed. "Here's where we live in Syracuse. It's in central New York. You will be traveling farther north." He waved his right hand over the whole map. "And see all this green area? See how big it is? This is all the Adirondack Park. There's six million acres of land in the park."

He continued, "Within the park are mountains. And if you look closely, you'll see that each mountain's name is written in black ink and marked with a black triangle. The abbreviation, Mtn, is next to each mountain's name. Can you see all the mountains?"

"What are those numbers below the mountain?" I asked.

"That's the elevation of each mountain," Dad's voice rose slightly, like when he gets excited. "Elevation means height. It's measured in feet, and all of the mountains in The Adirondacks are well over one thousand feet! The tallest is higher than five thousand feet. That mountain is

Marcy. Mount Marcy is the tallest in New York State. Its elevation is 5,344 feet. Isn't that incredible, Bella?"

My mouth opened, just as his phone rang and he left the room.

I'm standing on one leg pretending to be a pink flamingo when he returns. When it comes to balancing, I'm the absolute best!

I wonder aloud, "How many times have you camped in the Adirondacks?"

Dad shrugged. "I don't know, maybe a dozen. Pop took us when we were kids."

"What about Pop?" I asked.

"A lot more than me. He's camped with us and his friends for many years."

"Are you sure you can't come with us?" I pleaded.

"No. It's my weekend to close the restaurant. This will be a nice trip for you and Pop," he replied.

My father and my uncle own an Italian restaurant, and they take turns working on the weekends. My father is a chef, and he makes the best Fettuccine Alfredo. It's yummy!

This will be my first time away from my house in the nine years of my whole life. I'm nervous about leaving my father, but I hear my mother's voice telling me to be brave. I always hear her in my head.

KNOCK KNOCK KNOCK KNOCK KNOCK KNOCK

"POP!"

In two steps, he's hugging me. Hard.

"Are you all set, Bella?" Pop chuckled, releasing me.

He's a big balding man with gray hair and a kind smile.

"Yes!" I called back, running toward the stairs. "Let me grab my backpack."

When I returned, Dad and Pop were laughing about something. Dad gives me a kiss and hands me the road map.

"Have fun, Bella!" he grinned.

I like seeing him happy because he doesn't laugh and smile much anymore, but he just did. Twice!

"Okay, Bella. Let our camping adventure begin!" Pop said, whistling while loading a bag in his SUV.

I hand him my backpack. His one hand is reaching and pushing in my bag and backpack, while the other is closing the hatch. Piles of bags, a cooler, and things I've never seen before create a mound, and I can't see past any of it. I climb up in the backseat, squirming around, trying to get comfortable under the strap weight.

Chapter 2

My Cousin

"We're all gassed up. We just need to pick up Nash," Pop said, driving down our road.

I feel myself getting mad. I think my head is going to explode!

"What did you say?" My voice rises. Oh. It's definitely anger.

"Nash. He's coming with us," Pop explained.

"**Nash**?" I try to take a deep breath, but I can't. My eyes fill with tears. "POP! This is OUR first camping trip together. **You** said it was going to be OUR special time. Why does HE have to come? Why?"

Nash will ruin everything.

"I promised Aunt Mickey that Nash can join us," Pop explained.

"He's sooo D-U-L-L!" I yelled.

"ISABELLA!"

I think he thought that I was going to say that other "D" word.

"But he's altruistic!" I pleaded. I heard my parents talking about it one day.

"Autistic," Pop clarified.

"Yeah. That's what I said."

"Altruistic means that someone cares about other people. They're not selfish. Autistic means his brain works a little differently than yours, and he may communicate and interact in ways you're not used to. But he is extremely intelligent."

Communicating? That's true. Nash can't talk. I have never heard his voice. He hasn't spoken to me. Every summer, our large family has a reunion at Uncle Tony's house, where all the relatives gather. My cousins and uncles play games with me. Not Nash. He doesn't play with us. He never joins our activities. He just sits next to his mom or follows her around everywhere she goes. If she's inside, so is Nash. If she's outside, he is, too. He doesn't leave her side. I never played with him. He never even looked at me.

"Nash has gone camping with his family," Pop said. Pop's calm, but I'm not.

"He's camped and I haven't? He **can't** talk, but he's gone camping?" I questioned.

"Yes. He likes it. I think you're confusing communicating with knowledge. Nash is very intelligent. He's as smart as you."

"Pop," I paused. "I don't think so. Mrs. Stevens told Dad at my parent-teacher conference that I read above my grade level! I get all Es on my report cards! Nobody gets better than Es. He can't be as smart as me."

I boasted, "And how am I going to talk to someone **all weekend** who doesn't talk back?"

This trip is going to be awful! Just awful. I have to go camping with Nash! Boring — no talking, just like a baby — Nash! We're the same age, but he looks younger because he's smaller than me. He's camped and I haven't!

I just can't believe it! I really don't want to go with him. Another kid will be with me who won't even play with me!

Even though we live kind of close to each other, Nash and I go to different schools. I go to a private school. My school is a Catholic school that my father pays for. Nash goes to a public school. I wonder if he likes not wearing a uniform every day? It's not like I can *ask him*.

I wanted to tell Pop to turn his SUV around **right now!** But the truth is … I really want to go camping. I've been waiting all school year for this opportunity. School finally ended yesterday, it's the first day of summer vacation, and we're on our way!

Nash is short for Nashville. My Dad told me. It's a city in Tennessee. Tennessee is a southern state. Dad visited Nashville before, and he said thousands of musicians record their country music songs and live in Nashville. Mom liked listening to country music on the radio and CDs. I like it, too, because she did.

Pop ignored my pleas, and we pulled into Aunt Mickey's driveway. Her name is Michele, but they've called her Mickey since she was a kid. Dad and she are siblings, and Pop is their father. She has long, brown, curly hair and is shorter than Pop and Dad.

Pop gets out of the SUV first, greeting them. "Hey, Nash, Mickey."

As I get out, Aunt Mickey's grabbing me. Her hug is tight like Pop's, and I can feel her bones.

"Bella, I swear you are growing up so fast!" she laughed. "I haven't seen you since your mother's…."

I finished her sentence in my head. Funeral. It happens

all the time. People don't know what to say when your mom dies. My father is unsure what to say when we run into someone he knows. He changes the subject when this happens. It's difficult for him. He cries late at night when I'm supposed to be asleep. He doesn't know that I hear him.

"Nash is so excited about going with you," Aunt Mickey said while walking away.

Nash excited? He doesn't look excited. He's standing on his front porch next to his bags. He looks … terrified. In fact, he never looks up at Aunt Mickey. He's crying while she's speaking softly to him. I wonder what she's saying?

Pop placed Nash's backpack and bags in the back of the SUV, and I'm waiting for everything to crash down and tumble out of Pop's vehicle, but it doesn't happen. Pop opened the back door for me before walking around the front. Aunt Mickey is on Nash's side, attaching Nash's booster seat. Seriously? He's nine years old. I told you Nash was a baby.

"Why the car seat?" I asked. "Isn't he too **old** for that?"

"It's a long ride, and Nash doesn't weigh enough yet to just use the seatbelt," Aunt Mickey shrugged.

Nash climbed in and up while she attached his belt, gave him a hug, and quickly closed the door. There's no response from Nash.

"Here, Honey. I love you," Aunt Mickey whispered, handing him a tablet-looking thing through the open window. She handed Pop a white charging cord, and leaned in, kissing Nash's head.

"What's that?" I asked curiously, thinking it looked like an iPad but different.

"It's his device," Aunt Mickey looked over at me. "We call it his device, talker, or his voice. It's how he talks."

"He TALKS?" This news surprised me.

"He communicates through this. He uses it to tell us what he needs. It talks for him."

"Will he ever REALLY talk?"

She lowered her head and whispered, "I don't know."

She paused and spoke again, louder, "Don't worry, Bella. Nash knows how to use it. Just talk to him like you do with all kids. He understands everything you say. Maybe you can learn how to use it, too, and you can communicate back and forth with Nash. Have fun, you two!"

Fun? With Nash? Is she serious?

Chapter 3

The Long Ride

"Pop, how long is the trip?" I asked.

"Three hours," he said.

Three hours? That's forever! Three hours with Nash. Who is going to talk to me? Nash has been staring at the floor since we drove off. What's he looking at down there? Now he's crying softly again. This is going to be one long weekend! Pop's just driving. Doesn't he realize that Nash is crying back here? What a baby!

Houses and farms whip by us.

"Can you see the lake, kids?" Pop asked.

"Where?" I responded.

"Over on the left. Behind those houses. Keep looking. It appears and disappears as we drive. That's Oneida Lake."

"Are we there? Is that the Adirondacks?" I questioned him.

Pop laughed, "No. We have a while until we get there. We just started our trip. Bella, look at the map your father gave you."

I forgot how noisy Pop can be. He talks loudly. Dad said that Pop's hearing is going, but I'm not sure where it's going.

Nash stopped crying and hummed some tune. What is it?

The map's stuck under his booster seat. I tugged and tugged with both hands, and I heard it rip.

I'm mad that Nash's booster seat ripped it. It's all his fault.

"Oh No! Dad's map tore!" I exclaimed.

"It's okay. Don't worry. He won't mind. Some people don't even use road maps anymore. Open it up," Pop replied.

My arms are outstretched, and the map's hanging over Nash's seat. It looks different.

"This isn't the same map Dad showed me earlier!" I huffed.

"What do you mean?" Pop asked, surprised.

"It has pictures and orange-colored maps on the side. It's different!" I screamed.

"Hmmm. Try flipping it over," he suggested.

The map's actually heavy as I lift it up, swinging and crossing my arms. Suddenly, the corner hits Nash's head as I try to turn it over.

He stops humming and gazes down toward my seat, but not up at me.

"Tell me what you see," Pop said.

"There's words on the left, and more words and charts on the top next to them," I explained anxiously.

"Oneida Lake should be in the middle," he confirmed.

"Is it big? It looks like a big lake. It's blue, but it's covered by charts."

"Charts?" he questioned.

"Wait! Lake On-Tar-Rio?" I sounded out the word just like my teacher, Mrs. Sanders, taught me in first grade.

He pronounced it slowly, "Lake On-tare-rio. It's one of the Great Lakes. Look below it. East. Yeah. Southeast of Lake Ontario. It should look a lot smaller than Lake Ontario. It's blue and oval-shaped. The writing is probably really small. That's Oneida Lake."

I remember when Mrs. Tyler taught us the Compass Rose with north, south, east, and west in second grade, so I use that knowledge to locate it.

"Got it! Found it! Oneida Lake," I boasted.

Nash leaned toward the map, looking directly at it while humming. I lift the left side, so he can't see it. What would he know about maps?

"And all of this green is the Adirondacks," I said proudly to Pop, looking toward Nash. "Dad showed me this morning."

"Okay. Here's a question for you," Pop asked. "If we just passed Oneida Lake, which direction are the Adirondacks?"

I bet Nash doesn't even know what a map is.

"North," I answered, sticking my tongue out at Nash and mouthing the words, "I'm smarter than you!"

"North what?" Pop persisted.

"Northeast," I replied, giving Nash a wicked smile.

I'm so pleased with myself that I began closing the map. It's hard to fold, and I kept trying different ways. I struggled folding it back once in the middle and under on the bottom. It formed a smaller square, and I left the green of the Adirondacks showing. I stared at the map for a really long time, when suddenly I wanted to write in my journal. Shoot! My journal is in my backpack in the huge pile behind us.

"Pop, can you pull over and get my journal from the back?" I asked,

"Not now. When we stop, I will," he answered.

"But I want it. Now," I insisted.

"No."

I wanted to protest, but I know better than to ask Pop twice. I can't write, so I listen to the humming sound of Nash trying to figure out the familiar tune.

"Pop! Look at that HUGE farm."

Nash's neck tilted, and he looked over to my side window. Pop pointed out sights as he drove from country roads to highways and back to country roads. Did you know that another name for country is rural? We learned that in Mrs. Prince's kindergarten class.

"When we get there, we'll have to set up our camp right away," Pop yelled back to us. "It's better to have it done early because it takes a while. The last thing you want to do is set up camp when it's starting to get dark."

It felt like we rode in Pop's SUV for days. The bumpy road made my stomach feel weird.

"tree tree tree tree tree tree tree tree tree tree"

What was that? Nash's finger is bouncing up and down pressing a button on his "talker." When he presses it, a voice says the word **tree**. I glanced over. The button has a picture of a tree on it. He's right. All we can see on both sides of the road are trees. He's hitting that button so much that it's becoming ANNOYING!

Pop slowed down, and we pulled into a gas station. The town sign read Holland Patent.

"I'm going to use the bathroom, and so are you two," Pop warned, getting out of the SUV. "Don't say that you don't have to go. Just TRY!"

Nash is unbuckled and outside before me. How did he know how to do that? We all take turns using the one-toilet bathroom in the corner of the convenience store. I'm surprised that Baby Nash went in by himself!

Pop bought a newspaper, matches, hot dogs, rolls, long sticks, a box of doughnuts, ice, bug spray, batteries, and a small shiny square-looking thing he slips in his pocket. After paying the friendly woman behind the counter, we left. He opened the back of his SUV, and surprisingly, nothing fell out! Pop rearranged some items before opening the large cooler, dumping the bag of ice, and mixing it all up with his hand, covering the hot dogs and water bottles that were already in there.

"Why don't you grab a couple of those chocolate chip cookies?" Pop said, wiping his hands with a paper towel.

My stomach growled at the sight of them. My nonna bakes the best huge chocolatey chocolate chip cookies you've ever tasted! She bakes and cooks a lot. Everything is delicious. She can even make vegetables taste good. Truly, she can! She cooks at home and at the restaurant. She hardly leaves the kitchen.

"Pop, why didn't Nonna come with us?" I asked.

He laughed, "She doesn't like camping. She prefers hotels. I used to go camping with my friends, and she stayed home for the weekend."

She didn't come, but she baked for us. Thank you, Nonna!

"Try not to drink too much. We're not going to stop and use the bathroom again until we get there," Pop said.

The three of us stand silently eating cookies and taking only sips of water.

"Nash eats cookies?" I asked Pop.

"Of course," Pop replied, smiling.

"Bella, Nash has his device to communicate, but he is NO different than you!"

I nod, showing Pop that I understand, but I'm not sure that I do.

"Oh, can you grab my pink backpack so I can have it for the rest of the ride?" I asked.

He reached in and handed it to me. Now I can write in my furry pink journal!

Nash and I climbed back up into the SUV, and Pop helped Nash fasten his booster belt. The road turned hilly and winding, and there were a lot of farms on both sides of it. The trip is long and boring, so I wrote about taking Nash on our trip and describing everything I see on the side of the road.

"What are those huge gray things, Pop?" I asked.

"Those are called solar farms. Not like a farm with animals and crops, but those solar panels use the sun's rays to produce electricity. Basically, the sun shines on the panel and converts the sun's energy to electricity. Then, the electricity is used to power things like lights."

I continued describing everything I saw in my journal. I'm not sure how much time has passed, but I'm in deep thought when I hear, **"HA HA HA HA HA HA HA HA"** Nash is using one finger on his device and giggling. I see a white keyboard, and as he types, the louder he giggles.

"What's so funny?" I asked.

"HA HA HA HA HA HA"

He repeats it over and over, faster and faster.

"Stop it, Nash!" I said.

He keeps giggling and pushing on the iPad. It's **SO** annoying, but I'm grateful that his humming has ended.

We passed farms with red barns, small stores, churches with tall steeples, bridges crossing rivers, and signs. I'm reading all of the different kinds of signs on both sides of the road. There's Boonville, Deer Crossing: 4 miles, No Passing Zone, Route 28 North.

Pop pulled into a parking lot and told us to look up.

Nash typed, **"CRASH CRASH"**

It's an airplane coming out of a roof!

"We can get out and look," Pop suggested.

"The plane crashed right into the roof!" I shouted.

"It's not real, but it certainly looks like it, doesn't it?" Pop asked.

We got out and stared at it. Nash's arms and hands rose, and he jumped up and down.

"Do you like it?" Pop asked Nash, laughing. "Your

mother told me that this is one of your favorite things to see in the Adirondacks."

Nash took a picture with his iPad of the dark brown, almost black log building with a sign that read, THE WIGWAM. He takes a picture with his iPad, which surprised me. I realized that The Wigwam is a restaurant because a sign on the side of it lists soups, pizza, and burgers. There's a carved wooden door, and it has the back of a plane sticking out of the roof. We continued staring at it.

Pop broke our silence, "That's called the tail of the plane."

Nash is typing again — **J1MQ1** — that's the number painted in green on the plane's white tail. There's also a W in the middle of a green circle on the very back of it.

"It didn't really crash," Pop explained. "This is a fake plane that was built on the roof to look real. See those support cables that look like strings attached to the roof? Those secure it to the roof because of heavy snow and wind during the winter. All planes have a number on them to identify them. That number makes it appear real."

Pop should know. His brother is an airline pilot who also owns his own plane.

THE WIGWAM

Chapter 4

The Blue Line

We're back on the road when Pop slowed down and pointed out a sign that read *Entering Adirondack Park* hanging down from a wooden post.

"Look, kids. That sign shows visitors that they have entered the park," Pop said.

"It's a weird shape!" I exclaimed.

"Not really. It's shaped in the form of the entire Adirondack Park. Bella, if you look at your map, you'll notice that the map and the sign are the exact same shape."

Pop continued talking and driving. "Now we're inside the Blue Line."

"Where? Where's the blue line?" I asked.

"You can't see it," he chuckled. "The Blue Line is what the residents call the Adirondack Park."

"Residents? People don't live in parks!" I said.

"Yes. Residents," he replied.

He continued, "This is not like the park you go and play in. It's called a park and it's HUGE! People own businesses, houses, and camps in the woods and on the lakes, and live within the park. There's restaurants, stores, and hotels, too! The first Adirondack lake we see on this road is White Lake. It's coming up just ahead," he paused. "Look! You can see it to the left through the trees. In fact, I'm going to pull over to get some firewood."

There's this wooden structure with all these square dividers. Each square has pieces of wood in it. It reminded me of our classroom mailboxes. We all have one with our assigned number on each slot. This one has at least thirty slots in it. I just multiplied. Yes. Thirty.

There's a handwritten sign that reads *$6 per square*. Pop's wearing thick gloves, emptying the wood out of one slot, and carrying an armful. Nash and I watched him as he made a couple trips back and forth to his SUV to the set of wooden boxes.

"All campers have to stop at different places within the park to buy wood because you can't bring firewood into the Adirondacks. Any wood from outside the park might have insects in it. These invasive pests could spread, eating and killing all the trees. That would be devastating, so the wood that you use has to be cut from within the park. It has been dried, chopped, and is free of these pests. Each of those wooden squares has about eight to ten logs in it," Pop explained.

The drive took forever, and I continued writing in my journal while Nash looked out his window. I glanced up to see hundreds of trees buzzing by us. There are even houses hiding behind trees, and people actually live within all those trees. Their backyards are forests! I'm reading all kinds of signs: Scenic Byway, Deer Crossing, and even a picture of people with a backpack on.

Pop interrupted my thoughts, "See those signs? Those are hiking trails, and see those cars on the side of the road? Those belong to the hikers. They are hiking up a mountain now. Once in a while, you'll notice small parking lots, but a lot of hikers just pull over on the side of the road."

He pointed to the left side of the road. "Look! Look!"

I've read about dams, but I've never seen one. It's right there in the wilderness! Even Nash looked interested.

Beavers build dams to stop water and create a safe pond to build their homes. Their homes are called lodges. First, beavers use their teeth to gnaw through trees and branches, making the logs smaller. Then, they swim carrying the smaller logs, branches, and sticks through the water because it's easier for them to move in the water. Next, the whole beaver family helps to weave the wood using their mouths and hands. After, they dive to the bottom and bring up mud to put between the logs to make them stronger. We learned all that in kindergarten from a video we watched.

The ones we see don't look like a dam because they seem to be spaced apart. They must be lodges. Lodges are built similarly but have a couple underwater entrances on the bottom to swim up into and out of to escape predators. To me, it looks like a log teepee sticking out of the water.

We pulled off the road into a parking lot to look at a long, dark gray train. **Adirondack Scenic Railroad** is written on the side of it. Another sign reads Thendara.

"Are we going on a train the rest of the way?" I asked.

Nash types, **"train train train"**

"No, Nash. Not today. Maybe we can come back another time. We're going to drive.

We have about a half hour to go," Pop said.

"train train train" Nash continues repeating until we pull back onto the road.

Pop chats nonstop, pointing out restaurants and stores as we continue down winding roads.

"That's the town of Old Forge." We drive farther, "There's Inlet. See. There's more cars on the side of the road. They belong to hikers."

As Pop described the scenery, I'm reading the sign on the side of the road: Bald Mountain Trail. It says Mtn, and Pop explains the abbreviation to us, and that Mtn means mountain. I already knew that because my father pointed that out on the map this morning. The gigantic trees on both sides of the road are close together, and the woods look black.

"Pop, it's really dark in there. Do you think there's bears and moose right back there?" I pointed.

"It's possible. We are in the Adirondacks, and they both live within the park," he said.

"Have you seen any bears or moose up here?" I asked.

"There's black bears in the park. I **have** seen a black bear way off on the side of the road near Blue Mountain Lake, but I have never seen a moose. I'd like to, but only from a safe distance! I know you love animals, but remember, never approach or try to *pet* any wildlife," Pop exclaimed.

I would like to see a bear way off, just like Pop. Nash hums that song again.

"Here we are," Pop announced.

Finally!! We all got out and followed Pop. Beyond the cars, I see water, and I quickly count the boats. Ten. The lake is right there! Nash jumped up and down.

"Look!" Pop pointed, "That's Raquette Lake, and do you see it? That's Big Island where we are going, and the mountain to the left is West Mountain, and the other mountain over there is Blue Mountain."

This view of gray-blue water, green trees, and a mountain looks like one of the paintings on Pop's living room wall.

Chapter 5

Raquette Lake

We walked across the parking lot, and it sounded loud like the crunching of my morning cereal.

Pop shook some guy's hand, and he introduced us to Lenny, who owns the marina. They talked about boring adult stuff like families and work. Nash and I gazed across the water to the island. We heard people's voices in nearby boats.

Some tall man with blonde hair filled red cans with gas from one pump right at the end of the dock. It's really weird seeing a gas pump next to a lake!

Pop backed his vehicle up, and he unloaded the items he bought in the store first. He put an ADK sticker on his back window. So that's what he bought!

"We have arrived in the Adirondacks. Let's make it official," he announced, placing the sticker on his back window.

"What's ADK?" I asked.

"ADK is short for the Adirondacks. It's the abbreviation."

He seemed excited about the sticker. Maybe for Christmas, Dad and I can get him a sticker book. He handed us items to carry to the boat. Our hands are full unloading the SUV and walking back and forth between the dock.

"Is that our boat?" I asked. "It looks small."

Pop replied, "Yes, and it's a perfect size for us. It's called a skiff."

Nash and I placed our backpacks and sleeping bags in the skiff. The small skiff is metal with a tan carpeted floor. Pop lifted in the heavier items, like the cooler and tent. It took a long time to load everything. Do we really need all this? Finally, we moved the SUV to the last empty parking spot and walked back to the dock. Lenny handed Pop vests.

"Here. Put on a life vest," Pop commanded as he pulled on the straps at my waist, buckling the top and turning toward Nash to fasten and adjust his. Finally, Pop put his own vest on as he stumbled and stepped into the boat. He grabbed Nash's and then my hand as we stepped into the skiff, too.

"Sit down and stay seated until we stop and I tell you to stand," Pop instructed, pointing to a flat metal bench seat. One for us to share and one for Pop to drive the skiff. Our bodies swayed until we sat. I noticed another longer seat in the back. There are no seatbelts to strap us in, and our belongings take up a lot of space. On the shore to the right, other boats are tied to docks.

"Are you ready, kids? Hold onto your seats!" Pop said, pulling the cord a couple times until the motor coughed to life.

"Yes!" I screamed, lifting both arms up. Nash lifted his arms, too, but he was silent.

Pop had one hand on a black stick and one on the steering wheel. There's chug, chug, chugging from the motor as we coast from the dock.

"What is that?" I said, pointing down at the skiff floor.

Pop yelled over the motor sound, "That's an oar in case the engine doesn't work. I could row this skiff just like a rowboat." He paused, "Not that I want to. As we look around the corner to the right, you'll see Blue Mountain in the distance."

It is blue. Bluer than the water and the trees below it. We're picking up speed, and the wind blew my hair as the water slapped the sides of the skiff.

Nash covered his ears as we bounced along faster and faster. Cold water sprayed our faces and splashed our arms. I turn my head around, looking back. Water is rushing out of the bottom of the engine and forms a murky trail behind us as we get farther and farther from the marina.

Pop's head turned from side to side. "People are safe, but you should always look around for other boaters." He pointed, "That's Big Island."

The island went on and on as far as I could see. Huge boulders and towering trees transformed the water into a huge gray and green mirror. Big Island got closer and closer as our skiff approached the shoreline. Pop turned off the motor, and it's noticeably quieter.

Nash removed his hands from his ears as we glided in slowly. Pop stood, climbed over our stuff, and tipped the engine up.

"The water is shallow, so we don't want the propeller

to hit the rocks at the bottom of the lake. If that happens, the motor won't work. That won't be good," he explained.

Pop jumped out, grabbed the rope in the front, and pulled the skiff closer to shore. Nash made a grunting sound, pointing at the small fish swimming below us. The water was so clear that we saw straight down to the sandy bottom! If I put my hand in the water, I probably could touch the fish. But I won't.

Pop swung the rope around one of the sprawling tree roots, pulled it tightly, knotted it, and secured the skiff. Next, he lifted up the cooler, tent, and chairs, placing them on the ground. I quickly stood up to get out of the boat.

"Sit down, Bella. Nash is going first," Pop said.

"Why? I want to get out first!" I protested, wondering why Nash got to go before me.

"Nash, put your device on," Pop instructed, ignoring me.

Nash lifted his device and strap over his head, crossing it sideways over his shoulder and under his right arm. Pop pointed, telling Nash where to put his hands and feet as he climbed out of the boat and onto the rock. He used the tree root stairs along the bank side. Once Nash was up, it was my turn for Pop's instructions.

"Do you think you two can grab both ends of the cooler?" Pop directed us, "Drag them over a little, so we have more room to empty the skiff."

"Sure, Pop," I agreed as he handed up our backpacks and numerous bags of camping items.

We placed everything on the ground, and once the

boat was emptied, the three of us put on our backpacks and walked through the towering trees. I'm really strong, and I'm definitely stronger than Nash because I'm taller and bigger than he is.

Pop's ahead of us with full arms holding the tent and chairs, as he walked briskly over reddish-brown leftover fall leaves, small gray rocks, and tiny green ferns.

"Lift it! Nash! Jeez. Do I have to do it by myself? Come on!" I huffed, knowing Pop couldn't hear me. I still don't know why Nash even had to come with us on this camping trip.

The cooler had a handle and wheels, and I'm pulling while Nash is pushing the back of it through the brown dirt and scattered green moss. The hard ground crackled as the cooler crushed twigs, bark pieces, and leaves. I thought about my backyard and how different the ground looked and sounded compared to the silent, soft, velvety green grass under my bare summer feet.

Pop looked back and noticed Nash struggling.

"Leave that. I'll come back for it. There's a lean-to! I'm glad it's available. If not, we would have to put our tent on the ground," Pop shouted.

"There's no side," I mentioned.

"Sure, there is. There's three sides," Pop replied.

"Where's the door?" I asked.

Pop chuckled, "There's no door. The roof will protect us if it rains or if it's windy, and it's open so we can feel a breeze. We can also feel the warmth of the fire at night."

The rectangular lean-to looked like a small log cabin

with a longer back log wall and shorter side log walls. A wooden roof slanted toward the back wall, with the front part open. A few feet in front of it is a circle of piled stones. I'm staring at it, and I hear Nash's device, **"fire fire fire"**

"That's the fire pit, but we're not lighting it yet, Nash," Pop said. "Let's finish bringing everything over."

All at once, we're busy walking back and forth hauling all of the items that we took out of the skiff. Pop barked out orders to pick something up, carry it, and place it near or in the lean-to. He's like an Army sergeant, and Nash and I are his loyal soldiers; quiet, focused, and listening to each direction Pop gave, pointing here and there to place an item in a certain spot or unpack something. There's a lot of stuff to put away!

First, we set up the tent *inside* on the floor of the lean-to. Pop untied the tent, and it popped open (that was awesome) while he assembled the poles as the tent took shape.

Next, we unrolled and placed our sleeping bags and pillows inside the tent. Pop put his sleeping bag between mine and Nash's. I think he's doing that in case Nash happens to get scared in the middle of the night. Nash immediately crawled in and lay down, looking up at the tent roof. If he's doing it, so am I.

There's actually a lot of room in the tent. The sun illuminated the white cloth sides. Nash reaches up, and I do, too, touching the silky smooth dark blue roof. It's kinda like the blanket fort my dad and I made once under the kitchen table. Nash stared at the roof and giggled. I think of my father as I rush to the opening before Nash.

"Pop, can I call Dad and tell him that we got here?" I asked.

Pop sighed, "No. My phone doesn't work. There's no service on the island."

"WHAT? What about playing games or searching on your phone? No Wi-Fi? You're kidding, right?" I asked.

"No. Nothing. Isn't it great? There's no interruptions or distractions. It's just us and nature." Pop said.

I looked at him, puzzled.

"I'm serious. The phone doesn't work here and a lot of places in the Adirondacks," Pop confirmed. "We have a lot to do, so let's get to it."

He called Nash, "Out of the tent, Nash. We have more to do."

"Bella, open up those chairs and put them over there near that fire pit, but not too close. Closer. There." He pointed over toward the left, "Nash, go and get small branches and twigs to start our campfire."

"I can go, Pop," I said.

"No. He's got it," he replied.

"Why can't I?" I asked.

"Bella, you will have plenty to help with, too," Pop said.

Nash hurried back and forth gathering the kindling wood, and I put flashlights into the inside tent pouches and placed a lantern and our backpacks in the lean-to just as Pop instructed. Then, I followed his orders to hang our life vests on the inside lean-to pegs. I got on my tippy-toes and placed sunscreen and bug spray on the back wall shelf.

After we unpacked and set up the lean-to, Pop told us, "Tomorrow we'll walk around the island and take the boat out on the lake. Let's take a walk, and I'll show you what's around this area."

We walked behind Pop, and I saw a wooden structure ahead of us.

"What's that?" I inquired.

"I'm glad you asked because that's where we are headed," he said, stopping in front of it. "This is an out-house." He continued to smile, "This is where we'll go to the bathroom."

Nash looked over at me. They both did, as if there's some secret that they knew and I didn't. Pop opened the creaking, hinged wooden door. Flies revolted quickly, fleeing from their imprisonment. I could smell why, and I would escape from that odor, too.

Pop pointed to the white toilet seat with the lid up. "When you have to **go,** you use that hanging toilet paper and sit down there. I'll have to remember to bring some of our own toilet paper inside, or replace it, so nobody ever has to run out. It's good to be courteous and think of the next campers."

I wondered, "What other campers? You know we haven't seen anyone. Is anybody else on this island?"

"Yes. There's other lean-tos, campsites, and places to put up a tent on other parts of the island, but not a lot. We were lucky to get this spot facing the land and ma-rina. You can't reserve a campsite on the island like other campgrounds in the Adirondacks. It's on a first-come ba-sis. That means whoever finds a campsite or lean-to, it belongs to them for as long as they're here. Nobody can take our lean-to until we pack up and leave."

I nodded my head and peeked inside this outhouse. There are small openings on the top of the side walls that look like six tiny square windows. I gagged. It smelled like the worst dog doo mixed with spoiled milk.

Pointing up, I asked, "What are those holes?"

"That's for ventilation. To air it out. It's like a window," Pop explained.

"Well, they're not working very well, are they?" I asked, and Pop chuckled.

Cobwebs hung from the ceiling to the back and side walls, dangling like the ropes from my school's gym ceiling.

I noticed everything it's missing. "I don't see a handle to flush, or a sink to wash my hands," I said.

"No. There's no plumbing. Just a hole in the ground," Pop replied. "You can use sanitizer, or wash your hands in the lake." He pointed, "Actually, it looks like someone left some sanitizer in there."

Meanwhile, I'm thinking about what's at the bottom of THAT hole. Gross. Really gross! All of a sudden, numerous animals appeared in my thoughts, just waiting around that dank hole, ready to jump up and attack while I'm sitting down.

Nervously, I said, "Do snakes like to slither around in the outhouse?"

"No. I've come to this island for over thirty years, and I have never seen a snake on this whole island," Pop confirmed.

I'm not sure whether he is serious or lying just to calm me down.

"What if I have to go in the middle of the night?" I asked, picturing the wild animals that might be lurking in the woods or waiting for me behind the closed door. I vowed to myself not to eat or drink until we're back on land, where our SUV is parked. I figured that if I don't eat or drink, then I won't need the outhouse.

"Just wake me, and we can walk over using flashlights. I'll tell you what. I'll go in there first and check the inside before you go in. Then I'll wait outside while you go in. Do either of you have to use it **now?"** Pop asked.

I'll never use it! Never ever! That's just what I'm thinking when Nash quickly stepped up, closing the door. Nash can use the bathroom on his own, like in the gas station, and he isn't afraid of the outhouse! In a few minutes, he opened the wooden door, and Pop squirted sanitizer on his hands. Pop always carries a small sanitizer in one of his pockets.

After that disgusting conversation, Pop walked us in the opposite direction from the outhouse, the lean-to, and the skiff until there was a clearing to the shoreline. We walked over bumpy, twiggy, and mossy ground. Dead, broken tree stumps were in our way, so we had to step over or around them. I noticed there's no clear path like at the Nature Center we stroll through near our house. My feet sank slightly as I walked along the spongy ground. Nash hums that song again. It's so familiar. It sounds like a restaurant ad on TV.

Through the trees, I glimpsed sunlight glistening on the rippling water. A boat motor roared in the distance. We stopped at a small beach. Just below us, mossy boulders and smaller rocks appeared on the shore. Grass popped out of the clear, shallow water toward one side. Nash jumped up and down, again.

"That's where we will go swimming. Not now, Nash," Pop said. "Let's go start the fire, so we can think about eating. I bet you kids are starving."

Hungry? I vowed not to eat or drink while we're on this island!

◆ ◆ ◆

When we returned to the lean-to, Pop said, "Let's start the fire. First, we put in the kindling that Nash already found. Good job finding it, Nash!"

Did Nash just smile?

"Bella, in case you go looking next time, you can locate any dried-out branches or twigs from fallen dead trees. The drier the better. Now go get those newspapers from the blue hanging bag. We'll crinkle them up in our hands and put the twigs on top of the crinkled paper," Pop instructed.

We watched him. He used a long lighter just like my father uses for our grill.

"I'm going to light the corners of the paper. You two stay back and watch. The paper ignites the twigs, and they crackle. Then the flames get bigger and bigger. I'll add a small log from the bundle that I bought on the side of the road. After, I'll poke with this sturdy stick, and as the fire rises, I'll add another log," Pop said.

It took a while, and we watched him slowly and carefully bring the fire to life before he placed the grate over it.

"Every camper uses and leaves these grates next to the firepit for the next camper," Pop explained.

Once the fire ignited, he sprayed butter on a frying pan and put three hot dogs in it. He placed the frying pan on the grate, turning the hot dogs over and over.

Pop told Nash to talk on this device to choose his condiments between mustard and ketchup. Then, Pop asked for his drink choices of soda or water.

The device spoke, **"want cola" "want mustard."**

Pop smiled and thanked him for choosing, and guess what? Nash chose the exact same food choices as me. We both ate a hot dog on a roll with mustard, potato chips, and Pop gave me a choice of soda or water. I chose soda because Dad doesn't let me drink it at home.

"Pop, this is my first meal camping," I said.

"Yes. I suppose it is, Bella," Pop agreed.

I was hungry, and dinner tasted delicious even though I promised myself that I wouldn't eat or drink because of that smelly outhouse.

Nash quietly stared out toward the water. He hasn't cried since we got here! He is so quiet. Actually, it's kind of nice having a companion that doesn't talk your ear off! There was this girl in my class last year who **never** stopped talking. The teacher always had to remind her during the day.

For dessert, we had doughnuts, and we each took turns changing into our bathing suits behind a tarp that Pop hung up earlier for privacy. It reminded me of a store fitting room, the way the tarp opened and closed, hanging from a line similar to the one Nonna had in her basement for drying wet laundry.

When we changed into our bathing suits, we grabbed towels and walked down to the same beach that Pop pointed out earlier.

"Pop, you didn't give us Floaties to swim! Dad would never let me go in the lake without Floaties. Ever!" I shouted.

"No Floaties. We're not going out far. The lake is shallow where I'm taking you," Pop stopped walking. "This is where we can swim, wash our hands, or bathe. I have soap, if you want to bathe in the lake tomorrow or during the weekend."

"Bathe?" I asked.

Pop clarified, "Yes. You can swim and clean up at the same time. That's what you do when you camp. There's no showers or bathtubs here!"

No way. There's fish, mud, and seaweed in that lake. How clean can I get? No toys, either. I still have the same plastic floating bear that I used as a toddler, but I would never tell anyone because I'm **too** old for bath toys. That bear reminds me of my mother singing nursery rhymes to me as she washed my hair under the tub faucet. I squeezed that bear while her sweet voice described Mary and her pet lamb; her long fingers wound up in my tangles.

Biting my lower lip, holding back tears, I said, "Dad told me we would be swimming in the lake. He also said I could wait a couple days to shower till I get home."

I don't want Nash to see me cry.

"That's fine," Pop shrugged, stepping over and down the tree roots until his booted feet were on the sandy bottom. He traded his hiking boots for a pair of rubber shoes he carried.

"It's shallow, so I'm going out first to show you how deep it actually is and how far we're going into the lake," he pointed, facing us. "See this? You can swim in this whole area in front of me, but you can't go past me. Come on in!"

Nash followed in bare feet and walked out until he was shoulder high. Next, I slowly walked in deeper and deeper until the top of my legs were totally submerged.

"It's cold!" I screamed, feeling the pebbled sand under my tippy toes. I didn't dare dive under the frigid water.

"Nah. Come in farther. You'll get used to it. Look at Nash," Pop reassured me.

Nash's arms moved, and his feet kicked. I had to show Pop that if Nash could do something, I could do it better! I didn't go in that much farther, but I swam like this for a while, bobbing up and down on my feet.

Pop complimented Nash, "Look at you go!"

"Look at me, Pop! Look at me swimming!" I exclaimed.

"I see, Bella," Pop said. "You're doing great!"

I thought about how this was the coldest water that I ever swam in! I hated to admit it, but Nash did swim better than me. He was splashing around, and I followed beside him. If it wasn't for me being jealous that Nash swam better, I would be wrapped in my fluffy towel on shore, protesting that I would **never** go back into this Arctic Raquette Lake!

We swam for some time like this until Pop told us to get out, then we dried off, put on our sneakers, and started walking back toward our lean-to.

"Can both of you look for really long, thin branches, so we can use them for roasting marshmallows on the fire?" Pop challenged.

We searched, picking up branches.

"How's this one? Is this long enough? What about this?" I asked over and over.

Pop claimed most of them were too short or too skinny. He didn't reject any of Nash's, and he had a few branches in each hand. How come Nash's were better than mine? Pop probably didn't want to hurt Nash's feelings or see him cry, *again.*

Finally, Pop approved the best three. When we went back to the lean-to, we each took turns changing into dry clothes behind the tarp.

We hung our damp suits on pegs from the lean-to walls next to each other. Pop sat down in the middle of our two folding camp chairs in front of the lean-to, facing the fire pit. You could hear the voices of people zipping through the lake in their motorized boats. Looking beyond the tree openings, the water sparkled.

"Bella, can you get out the marshmallows, chocolate bars, and graham crackers?" Pop asked, pointing in the direction of a bag.

"Sure. Is it s'more time?" I replied, thinking that it wasn't even dark yet.

"Why not?" Pop said as I handed him the three ingredients. "Thank you. Can you open these?"

My long, wet ponytail dripped on the bag, box, and package as I tore the bag open. Nash and I stood on each side of Pop.

"Be careful when you put the marshmallow on. It goes on the end, and poke it right in the middle. It's easier with these larger marshmallows. Watch me," Pop continued, handing us each one, "Now turn the stick and keep turning it over the flames like this. You don't want it too burnt."

I looked over at Nash. He stared at Pop's hand, listening and turning his long branch at the precise moment that Pop did. When the marshmallow was light brown on each side, Pop held the graham crackers on both sides of the marshmallow. Then, with one hand, he quickly pulled off the marshmallow from the white gooey stick. Next, he opened the graham cracker sandwich, placing the chocolate bar in the middle between them. He laid it on the flat cloth armrest of his chair, and we took ours off, too.

"Careful. Don't burn your fingers," Pop warned.

Squirrels scampered around and birds sang in the trees towering over us, as we ate, peering out at the lake.

I broke the silence, pointing at the squirrels. "What kind of animals are on this island?"

"Hmm. Chipmunks, birds, rabbits, squirrels, and raccoons." Pop paused, "Oh. One summer, there was a deer on the island, but it probably walked across the lake in the winter on the ice and got stuck here until the spring when the lake thawed."

Nash typed the animals as Pop named them, and they repeated in the exact order on his device.

"chipmunk bird rabbit squirrel raccoon deer"

One s'more was enough, and I noticed that Nash didn't even finish his.

"Dad said that you've been camping for years," I mentioned.

"Yeah. Probably thirty-something. Most of the time, my buddies and I came here to the island, but we have camped at campgrounds, too. We preferred it here. It's so beautiful and peaceful. We have canoed, hiked up mountains and trails, and even biked here in The Adirondacks," Pop explained.

"Are we going to do all that this weekend?" I asked.

Pop laughed, "No. That's a lot for your first trip."

He stared into the fire, and Nash looked at his device.

I gazed into the fire, too, until I started to get bored, and I thought about writing in my journal.

I turned to Pop and pointed, "Can I go sit on that big rock by the lake?"

"Yes. As long as I can see you," Pop replied.

Chapter 6

Where's Nash?

I went into the lean-to, grabbed my journal, and walked over to the large rock. Pop waved from his chair. I sat, leaving my back toward Pop. The clearing opened up to a spectacular view of the lake. I could see why Pop loved coming here. I freed my pencil from my journal and began describing our earlier ride. Of course, Nash followed me over, standing near the water's edge, throwing small rocks toward the lake. He does a lot of things other kids do. Some rocks hit trees while others plunged into the water. He's humming that song, again.

"Nash, don't go any closer to the water. Stay right there," Pop warned, and Nash obeyed.

I was so engrossed in writing details and filling pages of our arrival at Big Island when I realized something was different. I stood abruptly, dropping my pink faux fur journal into the dried brown leaves scattered beneath me. I bent down and noticed the leaves stuck on the journal, so I quickly brushed them off with my right hand. It was quiet, and I glanced over at the area Nash was in. No rocks and no Nash! Our empty skiff to the right bobbed securely in the water. Where was Nash?

Turning around, I saw Pop sitting next to the fire in his camp chair. His eyes were closed and his head tilted back as he snored loudly. In an instant, my darting eyes scanned the lean-to, the open tent, and the whole surrounding area. Walking toward our campsite, I noticed Nash wasn't there either. His device was on the ground next to the corner of the lean-to, but where was **he**? Walking over, I grabbed it and placed it across my chest just like he wore it. Pop's snores grew louder as I ran toward the outhouse.

I called out, "Nash, are you in there? Nash?" I knocked. "Nash? Nash, answer me!"

Okay. Why did I just say that? He can't answer me. He can't speak, and he can't use his device because I have it.

"Nash? Nash? NASH! Make a noise if you can hear me!"

I knocked on the door and finally said, "Nash, I'm opening this door and coming in!"

And I did ... but he wasn't in there. It was just an empty, smelly outhouse with a white raised toilet seat and buzzing flies fleeing to freedom!

Instead of walking back to our lean-to, I headed down to where we swam earlier, but he wasn't there either. I briefly thought about running back to wake Pop, but dismissed that thought, fearing Pop would be mad at Nash for disappearing. Pop has a really deep, loud voice, and when he raises it, his yelling is scary. Really scary. The last thing Nash needed was to get scared. Why scare him? So far, Nash has had fun on this trip, and he hasn't cried on the island. Why should he start now? Pop's loud voice would definitely make Nash cry.

I have to find Nash! I traipsed off in the opposite direction of the lean-to and outhouse with the shoreline behind me. There wasn't a clear path to follow, so I just walked on, calling, "Nash, Nash."

The lake was no longer visible. I peered ahead and at the ground, glancing at my sneakers and wishing I had grabbed my rubber boots sitting on the lean-to floor. What if I stepped on something icky? Small ground holes appeared, and I wondered what kind of animal might be hiding beneath. Would a snake slither out? Light wind whistled through the trees. The brown ground changed from hard to spongy. It was littered with sticks, branches, and dried leaves. As my feet crunched on, I noticed green moss, mushrooms, ferns, and numerous trees resembling our annual family room Christmas tree. Some evergreens were so tiny that I couldn't help stepping on them, while others were as tall as me! Fifty-four inches. At least that's what the doctor told my dad at my last visit.

"Nash? Nash? NASH!" I called out every few minutes.

Bright green miniature cactus-looking plants shot up in clusters from the ground. I trekked around them, passing dead fallen trees and huge rotted tree trunks. The tree trunks were about waist high. Another tree trunk grew upward, curving over and above a moss-covered boulder. How strange it looked. Birds chirped, and I wondered if they could see Nash from their high perches. Trees and evergreens spread out before me. Their scented needles became stronger with each step. The bark on the other trees looked different. Some were whitish and some were brown.

A darker tree sky surrounded me. Taller grass appeared, and the ground over on the right shimmered. I turned, avoiding the area with water, and trudged through larger branches and stepped on and over fallen tree trunks. I stopped to listen for sounds, scanning the forest for any sign of Nash's navy T-shirt. Before long, it's eerily quiet with no sound of birds or squirrels.

As I walked on, I noticed that there was a dim light on Nash's device. I held it with my two hands, thinking that a little light might be helpful.

"NASH! NASH! Where are you?"

For the first time since I left the lean-to, I was worried. Really worried. I kept thinking of Nash regretting not going back and telling Pop. Maybe I shouldn't have thought of Pop yelling at Nash or Nash crying. Maybe he wouldn't have yelled at Nash at all. Even if he did, Nash would have stopped crying eventually, just like he did in the car on our way up here. So what if he cried? What if Nash was lost?

Lost without his Talker? Does he know how to scream? Is he capable of screaming for help if an animal or a stranger approached him?

Poor Nash. He's probably frightened. He is a kid and smaller than me. I may never see him again. Why am I thinking like this? This morning, I didn't care about Nash. In fact, I didn't want him to go with us. I wanted Pop all to myself. I called him a baby. Wait. Did I call him a baby out loud or to myself? Hopefully, I didn't say it aloud. That's not a nice thing to say. My dad would tell me that I should know better, and my mother would be disappointed.

Adults say that word all the time. Disappointed. All of my teachers used that word, too. Not to me, but to other kids. I never get in trouble at school. My thoughts turn to how I've been treating Nash. Pretty poorly, actually. I've ignored him all day. I talked to Pop, but not Nash. He didn't do anything to deserve it. Actually, he's been an okay companion. We prefer eating the same food. We like to swim. We have a few things in common. I'm thinking of all this when I notice that the forest is getting darker. Oh no! Is the sun going down? What time is it? How long have I searched for Nash? There's buzzing near my ears as I keep turning my head swiftly, swatting at pests that I can hear, but can't see.

Breathing deeply, like my counselor taught me, I yelled again, "Nash. Nash. NAAASH!"

Suddenly, I'm on the ground. I fell over one of the hundreds of tree roots.

"the the the the the"

Nash's device squawked; it activated when I fell. As I stood up, my ankle throbbed. Did I break it? Sprain it? A kid in my class had a bad sprain and missed a few days of school before hobbling back in. It really hurts. There's more buzzing around my head. I scratched my neck and leaned against a tree trunk. Oh No! What do I do now? I can't walk. Thinking about my ankle and how doomed I was made me cry. I can't find Nash, and now I'm lost in the dark with a broken ankle, too. I'm alone. Alone and scared.

I called out, again, but not for Nash. Not this time.

"Mommy."

"Mommy!"

"Mommmmy."

My soft weeping turned into louder sobs.

I called out to her over and over, knowing she couldn't answer me. Why couldn't she be here with me? She would know what to do. She always knew what to do. But the truth is, she will NEVER answer me, and I will never see her again. Not in person. Only in my sleeping dreams. I pictured her long, dark hair, smiling face, and sparkling black eyes looking back at me. My grief is huge. I sob louder, hardly catching my breath, walking deeper into the darkness; my ankle pain is starting to go away. My mother's healthier face morphed to her bald head, pale face, and sunken, dull eyes. The image haunting me in these black woods. I'll never forget the way she looked the last day I hugged her as I lay next to her bony body in that hard hospital bed. She whispered softly, struggling to speak, telling me she would always love me. She somehow got the word *proud* out, too. I knew the sentence that she couldn't say.

I miss her so much and wish she were here now. It wasn't fair that she was gone. It just wasn't! Why couldn't she have lived? I **need** my mother. The tears soaked my cheeks. Salty snot burned my lips and dripped into my mouth.

I'm trying to be brave like my mother always told me, but I can't stop my shaking body. I'm bawling so hard and loud that I almost miss the sound. Something moved over in the weeds. Sniffling, I froze, concentrating on the noises around me. I'm focusing and intensely becoming aware of that one sound. What is it? Pop told us deer, raccoons, rabbits, chipmunks, birds, and squirrels live on the island. Nash's device repeated those same animals earlier. I think about which of those animals were friendly and which were threatening. The raccoon could be mean and nasty. The raccoon is nocturnal and should be waking up soon. Hopefully, that was not the animal moving in the weeds. The soft hair on my arms stands up as I close my eyes, trembling with thoughts of an imminent raccoon attack.

Chapter 7

Found

The rustling sound through the brush gets louder. It sounds like something bigger than a raccoon. It's dark now. My thoughts turn from a raccoon to a Sasquatch. On the drive up, I noticed different Bigfoot cutout silhouettes in people's yards. Do they really live in the Adirondacks? Pop didn't mention it. Can they be on Big Island? I should have asked him about them!

My imagination envisions a huge Sasquatch hovering over Nash, holding him hostage. I pictured Nash's arms tied to one of these tall, thin trees, desperately trying to scream for help, but no sound came out. A fire burns at his feet as though he were a Salem witch. The image cleared as I heard something getting closer and closer until I jumped and screamed simultaneously. My jumping caused Nash's device around me to light up. The dark shadow walked toward me with each crackling step. I tightly closed my eyes, hoping it would disappear, but the anticipation popped them open just as the shadow stopped right in front of me. It wasn't huge or tall like Bigfoot. It was shorter than me.

"Hi!"

I shrieked, stepped back, but then I leaped forward, grabbing and hugging him. He stood with his arms at his side, but I just hugged him harder. He pulled away, and I released him.

"Wait. Did you just say *Hello*? Nash, can you talk?" I said, hugging him again. Now I'm bouncing up and down, realizing my ankle isn't sore anymore. His left hand reached out for his device around my neck.

"Oh yeah. Here," I said.

He typed, **"you cry"**

"Did you hear me? I was looking for you; I was so scared."

I continued, "I wanted my mother, and I was crying for her. She's dead. Did you know that? Do you understand what death is? It means that I will never see her again. It really stinks! It's so unfair."

I sighed, "You know what, Nash? I'm so glad that I found you, and we're together. I won't be as afraid with you here with me. I also appreciate you not telling me that it's okay, or that it's going to be okay. Adults have been saying that to me for a year. My teachers, my counselor, my mom's friends, my father, your mother, and Nonna. Even Pop!"

Nash stood still, and there was something comforting in his silence. I'm not sure if he understood what I was saying, but he patiently waited while I spoke.

I imitated a grown-up voice, "Bella, it's going to be okay. You're going to be okay." I paused, raising my voice, "The truth is that I'm NOT okay! I'm not going to be okay.

I think of my mother every day. ALL DAY! I miss her, and I especially want her when I'm frightened, like just now before I found you. She's not here to comfort me when I get scared. She's never going to be here when I need her."

I have never talked like this to anyone, and I think that I'm going to cry uncontrollably, again, but I don't. Instead, sniffling, I said, "But I guess I'm okay now that you're here. I'm glad you came with us today."

We just stood there for a moment, and I felt a sudden calmness there alone with Nash until his "voice" said, **"dark now"**

"I know. I kept searching for you, and now it's dark and we're lost. Where were you? Why did you leave?" Why am I questioning him?

"rabbit" his device replied.

"Rabbit? A rabbit?" I was puzzled. "Did you follow a rabbit?"

"Yeah," Nash said softly in his own voice, looking down at the ground.

"You spoke again!" But after that, he just stood there without responding.

I thought about how we were going to get out of there, and I knew that I needed to be brave and figure out a way back to our lean-to.

"I'm not sure where we are. Everything started looking the same, and it kept getting darker. We don't even have a flashlight!"

Nash made an indescribable sound, held up his device, and started walking. Using the light in front of him, he guided ahead as I followed in silence. Where's he going? Does he know the way back to the lean-to? How is he walking forward with so little light? He led, and I tripped a couple of times over unseen branches. Nash never stopped. He's moving as if the same spooky sounds I heard don't bother him. Again, I wondered if he knew which way to go and where he was leading us.

It occurred to me that maybe Nash wasn't lost at all. Pop said that Nash had camped before. Maybe Nash knew his way around Big Island. I kept up with him as he went faster and, without warning, glowing lights appeared up ahead.

"What is that?" I asked with no reply.

The lights appeared closer and brighter. A tall shadow followed the lights. Could it be? Is it the Sasquatch? I screamed, and Nash jumped, surprised by my loud squeal.

"Nash? Bella?"

"Pop! Pop!" I said, raising and waving my arms back and forth.

He was right in front of us, wearing a headlamp and carrying a lantern.

"Why did you leave the camp? BELLA?"

Uh oh. Pop's angry.

I had to think quickly, "I. I wanted to explore, and Nash followed me. I walked farther than I intended, and before I knew it, we were deeper in the woods, and it started getting darker."

"YOU SHOULDN'T HAVE LEFT THE CAMP WITHOUT

ME! What if you got hurt? There's marshy areas where you could sink down into the water, get stuck, or even drown." He didn't stop. "And you left in the evening when it gets dark! That was very irresponsible of you, and you dragged Nash along, too!" He paused, "Let's get back to camp. Stay close and follow me, and when we get back, we're going to talk about the consequences. You need a consequence!"

That can't be good. I wanted to say more, but I knew better than to talk when any adult was mad. Especially Pop. He led us, Nash was at his heels, and I followed the glow and shadows of the two of them. Pop knew these woods well, and in minutes we were back to the lean-to and the roaring and glowing fire of our campsite.

"Here," Pop handed us bottled water. "Drink."

He sat in his chair and pointed to the chairs to his sides.

"Sit!" He paused and then spoke, "Walking back, I thought of some consequences for your behavior, and I could only think of one solution. Bella, you did something serious and potentially threatening when you left me and the campsite."

Chapter 8

The Consequence

Pop raised his fingers one by one and sternly spoke, "First, you were impatient. I told you that we were going to do some exploring of the island tomorrow, but you couldn't wait. Why would you leave the campsite without me? Second, you were selfish, and you brought Nash with you into potential harm. Did you even **ask** him? Maybe he didn't want to come, but he just followed you because you're a kid. Third, you were unprepared for your exploration. You didn't know the area, and you had no flashlights! Luckily, you had Nash's device to give you a little light to walk with."

Should I mention that it was my idea to bring Nash's device, and that he left the lean-to without it? Should I blame Nash?

Pop continued, "Did you anticipate that inside the woods it's darker and that the sun would be going down? Good campers anticipate and think ahead. Here's a true fact: Hikers don't hike at dusk. They're either finished and down a mountain by then, or they are settled at their campsite just like we were. And finally, most importantly, you and Nash could have gotten hurt. What if you got hurt?"

Should I mention my ankle? I hurt it, but I don't say

a word. I'm as mute as Nash. I contemplate. Should I tell Pop the truth? Should I say it was Nash that wandered away? Should I tell him that I didn't want him to yell loudly at Nash, so I didn't wake him? Should I say anything to defend my actions?

I decided quickly, and I'm happy with what I chose.

I am **not** going to tell Pop that it was Nash who left, and I set off to find him. I am **not** going to explain that he has a really loud and scary voice, and I didn't want him to yell at Nash. I am **not** going to describe how Nash was the brave one and navigated us back in the right direction. I still don't know how he knew the way. I am **not** going to admit that I was constantly scared, and I even cried for my mother. No. I won't say a word.

"So, here's what I decided," Pop said. "We're going to wake up tomorrow, eat breakfast, pack up, and go home. We are not staying. This is your consequence, Bella."

He turned toward Nash, "I'm sorry about this, buddy."

Pop got up out of his chair to stoke the fire and put another log on it. Nash had no reaction to the news, but I sat stunned, and for the second time tonight, I cried. But this time, with my shoulders and head down, I whimpered softly. Pop was unaffected by my grief.

A small body came over and stood close to my camp chair. He understood. Nash was calm and brave tonight, and his presence comforted me. He brought us out of those dark woods. He is not a baby. Pop was right. Nash is no different than me. I stopped crying and looked over at him. He didn't look at me, and that was okay.

Chapter 9

Night

My eyes watered from the fire's acrid smoke circling around us. We ate some more of Nonna's chocolate chip cookies. Pop only spoke when I asked a question about particular sounds we heard. I thought if I kept asking questions, maybe Pop wouldn't be so angry. I couldn't stop talking.

"Why does the log make popping noises like that?" I asked.

"The logs have air pockets in them that cause it," Pop answered.

"What is that chirping?"

"Crickets."

Then I asked, "What's that?"

"That's the horn of the W.W. Durant dinner boat heading back to town for the night."

"Do you hear voices on the water?" I continued.

"Those are the voices of people on boats going back to their camps."

"What are those lights from?"

"The lights are from the marina, boats, buoy markers, and other camps. The lights far off to the right are lights from the town."

Dad says I'm inquisitive, which he says means curious, and Pop answered every question patiently.

Nash typed words that pertained to my questions.

"boat town light water people"

Pop **was** right. Nash **is** smart! He's as intelligent as me.

Pop stood up, got his headlamp and flashlights, and he handed us some, too.

"Follow me closely, we're going to the outhouse before bed," Pop said.

I didn't dare protest. We traipsed, again, over the crunchy ground toward the stinky wooden structure. This time, walking in the dark didn't seem so scary with Pop and Nash alongside me. Nash flashed his beam on the ground and up into the trees, repeating the pattern. Up. Down. Up. Down. Up, down, all the way toward the outhouse.

When we arrived, Pop went in first and told us not to move from our spot.

"Okay. I put in an extra light and looked around inside. There's no creatures in there. Bella, you go in, and then Nash could go after you. Make sure you GO," Pop said.

I reluctantly went in and urinated as quickly as humanly possible. I remembered my mother saying, "When you have to go, you have to go." This was one of those times.

"See, Bella. It's not scary in there," Pop said as he handed me the sanitizer.

It was unpleasant, but not that bad. "Nash, I'll hold your voice as you go in." I offered, extending my hand.

Pop smiled, "Nice, Bella."

When Nash came out, Pop handed him the sanitizer and went in to get the extra lantern. On our walk back, we heard voices and saw headlights from the boats returning to their camps around the lake.

Pop put more logs on the fire and hung the lanterns above our changing area.

"Do you two want to change into your pajamas?" Pop asked.

Pop and Nash kept their T-shirts and shorts on and didn't change into their pajamas, but I decided to change behind the tarp. I thought about Winnie the Pooh in my backpack, but I didn't get it. This time, I didn't want Nash to think *I* was a baby. Just then, Nash pulled a stuffed animal sloth out of his pack, so I went over and grabbed Pooh.

"Do you both have everything you need?" Pop asked.

Nash nodded, and I said, "Yes."

Pop turned the knobs off on the lantern in the lean-to, and the only light was from the campfire and the lantern he brought into the tent. Nash and I took turns zipping the two tent flaps. We crawled into our own sleeping bags on opposite sides of Pop. The lantern cast shadows on the side of the tent, and I started making shadow puppets. Nash copied me until Pop said, "Lights out. Time to sleep."

Pop turned the lantern off, and Nash's device dimly lit up his side of the tent.

"Goodnight, Bella and Nash," Pop said.

"Goodnight, Pop. Goodnight, Nash," I repeated.

"good night," Nash replied.

Immediately, Pop's snores echoed against the cloth sides, followed by the crackling fire sound. I peered over Pop and saw Nash using his device, but I couldn't hear anything. He must have turned down his volume.

Waves knocked against the island's shoreline, and faint voices echoed from camps across the lake. It took a while to fall asleep as the campfire popped and an owl hooted. I'm not sure if Nash was sleeping, but the last thing I remember was rolling over, cuddling Pooh, worrying about disappointing Pop, and thinking about my mother.

Chapter 10

Birds, Boats, and Breakfast

The dawn light filling the tent woke me. Nash was awake using his device, and I could hardly hear it talking back. The birds chirped and boat motors roared. I lightly touched Pop's shoulder.

"Pop, you're snoring," I said. "Loudly."

"Hmm. Okay. I'm awake," he replied, not moving. "Give me a minute."

Nash stared at his screen, grunted, and jabbed it into Pop's side.

Pop turned his head and squinted at the screen, "Oh yeah. It needs a charge. We will take care of that."

Pop yawned, sat up, and unzipped the tent. Cool air kissed my cheeks. We all exited the tent, climbing down from the lean-to. Light fog blanketed the lake.

I pointed, "Look, Nash, it looks like ghosts floating on water."

Standing next to me, Nash stared out at the water. There's a chill in the morning air, prompting my search for my favorite pink hoodie.

"That's mist coming off the lake," Pop explained. "It's from the warm water converging with the cold air of the night. As the sun shines on the water, the mist will disappear. You'll see."

"Why is my backpack wet?" I exclaimed.

Pop felt it. "That's just damp. Part of the nighttime dew that forms. It will evaporate soon, just like the lake mist. That's why we hung up most of our belongings. It happens at night when the temperature cools. It's part of camping. Look at the chairs!"

I took my backpack and dressed behind the tarp. I pulled my pink hoodie over my T-shirt. We walked to the outhouse. Now I am an Outhouser (my own new, made-up word) camper! The morning boat engines roared on the lake, and the birds were having a concert in their perches high above us.

When we returned, Pop asked, "Who's hungry?"

"I am!" I yelled, turning toward Nash. "Are you?"

"yes"

"Do you want eggs cooked over the fire or doughnuts?" Pop asked.

"doughnuts"

"I agree, Nash. Doughnuts, please!" I replied.

Pop poured us some milk from the cooler and handed us each a doughnut before he put a log on the fire.

"The mornings here are always cool," Pop said.

As I ate, I thought about how upset Pop was last night, and how much I wanted to stay here camping on the island

and play with Nash. I nervously waited for Pop to mention the consequence.

"I have been thinking about what I said last night about a consequence. I feel strongly that what you did, Bella, was wrong. I'm still disappointed in your irresponsible behavior and your bad choices. However, I have reconsidered, and I hope you learned from your mistake. Everyone is safe, and I think we should stick to our original plan and stay the weekend. I'm giving you a second chance. What do you think?" Pop asked.

I sprang up and ran over to hug Pop. "Let's stay. I am so sorry, Pop. I will never do something like that again. Never Ever!"

"What about Nash?" Pop asked. "What should you say to him?"

I turned to Nash. "And I'm sorry, Nash!"

Nash never looked at me.

"Apology accepted, Bella," Pop exclaimed, standing up and putting another log on the dying fire. Today, we'll explore the island and take a boat ride."

"Yay!" I shouted, hopping up and down. "What do you say, Nash?"

Nash hopped, too, and he pushed a button on his device.

"yes"

I giggled, "Okay, cousin, let our Big Island Adventures begin!"

Glossary According to Bella

CDs: CD stands for compact disc. A CD is round, plastic, and shiny. It plays music on a CD or DVD player.

Communication Device: An iPad or iPhone app that helps nonverbal children or adults communicate.

Compass rose: A circular flower-like diagram found on a map pointing to the direction of north, south, east, and west

COVID year: A virus broke out across the world that made many people very sick, and some even died. Schools across the United States and the world closed from March 2020 until the end of the school year. Students were sent home with computers and their teachers taught them remotely five days a week. Remotely means that the students watched their teachers live on the computer screen from the safety of their homes. Some schools stayed closed into the next school year, from September until December. My school opened back up in September of 2020.

Headlamp: This is like a flat flashlight you wear on a headband so you can have two free hands for making s'mores and doing campsite chores at night.

Lean-to: It's made out of wood like a cabin, but it only has three sides and an open front. If you look at it from the side, the roof leans back.

Outhouse: It's a wooden structure in the woods used as a toilet.

Outhouser: A word I invented for a person who uses an outhouse while camping.

Sasquatch: A very tall and really hairy creature that looks like a man. It's also called Bigfoot. Don't worry, they don't exist.

Some Questions From Bella to Think About Around the Campfire or at Home

Have you ever been camping before? If yes, what are some of your favorite things about it? If not, do you have favorite vacation activities?

Do you have any games you like to play on long car rides?

I learned Mount Marcy has the highest elevation (that means the tallest point) in New York. What's the tallest building or mountain near your home?

Do you know what kind of animals you'd find in the woods where you live?

If you got lost like Nash and I did, what is the first thing you would do?

Would you have interacted differently with Nash at first? How about after getting to know him better? Have you ever changed your mind and opinions about people?

Why do you think that Nash waited to speak to me? Do you think he's a little shy sometimes?

What if Pop didn't decide to forgive the consequence, and we went home early? Can you rewrite the ending?

Don't forget to join Nash and me in our next book, *Our First Camping Trip Day 2,* as we continue our Big Island weekend with Pop.

Acknowledgements

First, I would like to thank my husband, Glenn, for his love and support. He is my biggest cheerleader! He shared his three decades of Adirondack camping experiences and brought me out to Big Island. In the process, he turned me into a camper as well.

Secondly, a heartfelt thank you to Gina Noel, who spent time out of her laboring schedule creating and illustrating Bella and Nash's camping quest.

Also, my sincere gratitude to all of my fellow educators, colleagues, family, and friends (working and retired) who discussed, read, or helped polish the manuscript with suggestions from their individual knowledge and expertise. Many thanks and appreciation to Tricia Lee, Michele Rodolico, and Karen Ristau. I have to mention you, Jen. Thank you for the opportunity to volunteer in your classroom every week! You are all caring friends and gifted educators. You're also the sisters I never had.

In addition, I want to acknowledge my grandmother's neurodiverse second cousin, Charlie. Charlie was much older than me, but I can remember visiting him as a child, and his positivity and creativity were amazing. He was an inspiration.

Finally, a tremendous thank you to the incredible women at Wildebeest Publishing. They both supported the idea of this book and guided me through every step.

It wouldn't be possible without the sharp eye of Jess Neiding, editor and motivator, as well as Laura Thorne, advisor and mentor, who expertly polished the final result. Their patience, insight, and expertise were invaluable. Most importantly, the publishing process was enjoyable thanks to these two wild beasts!

About the Author

Kim Adams is an educator and storyteller who spent twenty-five years working with elementary school students, including those with neurodiverse needs. Her experiences in the classroom and her love of the outdoors inspire the adventures she writes for young readers. Kim lives in New York State with her husband, Glenn, where she enjoys hiking and exploring nature.

About the Artist

Gina Noel worked for thirty years in the banking and mortgage industry. In her spare time, she brought Bella and Nash to life with her charming illustrations. She is married with four children and ten grandchildren. She lives in New York State.